*ZURI*RAY*
Tries
Ballet

Written by **Tami Charles**

Illustrated by **Sharon Sordo**

Quill Tree Books
An Imprint of HarperCollinsPublishers

ROBOTICS

IT'S
SUMMER!

SPORTS CAMP

DRINK MORE
WATER

MAGIC CAMP

MUSIC
CONCERT!

To my niece, Laila Jones,
the Zuriest Zuri I'll ever know!
—T.C.

To Leo, for encouraging me to live my dreams.
—S.S.

Quill Tree Books is an imprint of HarperCollins Publishers.

Zuri Ray Tries Ballet
Copyright © 2021 by HarperCollins Publishers
All rights reserved. Manufactured in Italy.
No part of this book may be used or reproduced in any manner whatsoever
without written permission except in the case of brief quotations embodied in critical
articles and reviews. For information address HarperCollins Children's Books,
a division of HarperCollins Publishers, 195 Broadway, New York, NY 10007.
www.harpercollinscthildrens.com

Library of Congress Cataloging-in-Publication Data

Names: Charles, Tami, author. | Sordo, Sharon, illustrator.
Title: Zuri Ray tries ballet / written by Tami Charles ; illustrated by Sharon Sordo.
Description: First edition. | New York : Harper, [2021] | Audience: Ages 4–8. | Audience: Grades K–1. | Summary:
   Zuri Ray loves trying extraordinary new things but when Jessie, her Best Friend From Diapers, chooses
   ballet, Zuri Ray finds it too challenging until the teacher encourages her to be herself.
Identifiers: LCCN 2020013606 | ISBN 978-0-06-291489-7 (hardcover)
Subjects: CYAC: Individuality—Fiction. | Ballet dancing—Fiction. | Best friends—Fiction. | Friendship—Fiction. |
   African Americans—Fiction.
Classification: LCC PZ7.1.C4915 Zur 2021 | DDC [E]—dc23
LC record available at https://lccn.loc.gov/2020013606

The artist used Photoshop to create the digital illustrations for this book.
Typography by Rachel Zegar
21 22 23 24 25   RTLO   10 9 8 7 6 5 4 3 2 1
❖
First Edition

Zuri Ray wasn't your average kid.
She loved trying new things . . .
extraordinary things . . .
anything-but-ordinary things . . .
    Like . . .

Snorkeling with Mom.

Science experiments with Dad.

Ghost hunting with her big sister, Remi, and their pup, Sherlock Hound.

Zuri especially loved trying anything new with Jessie Colón, her BFFD—that's "best friend from diapers," in case you didn't know.

Zuri and Jessie took turns choosing activities. And they always thought each other's ideas were super cool.

But then . . .

. . . ballet camp happened. A whole week of it!

On the way to their first class, Jessie promised, "It will be *fabulous, dahling*!"

Dad agreed. "Don't worry. Just be yourself."

Zuri felt nervous, but she was ready for the challenge!

"Welcome, class! Places, please! I will demonstrate the five basic positions," Madame Adele said.

Zuri tried to be prim like Jessie.

And she tried to be proper like the other ballet dancers.

But her arms and legs had their own plans.

In the second class, Madame Adele said, "Today, we'll learn pirouettes."

Jessie twirled in perfect circles, with perfect, pointed fingers and toes . . .

But there was nothing *fabulous* or *dahling* about Zuri's pirouette.

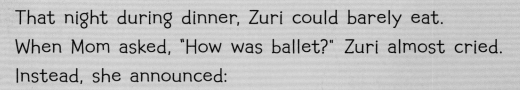

That night during dinner, Zuri could barely eat.

When Mom asked, "How was ballet?" Zuri almost cried.

Instead, she announced:

"I QUIT!"

"Why?" Remi asked.

"It's too hard for me," Zuri replied.

"You know what Dad says. When the going gets tough...
"The Rays get *tougher*," Zuri whispered, and smiled.
Zuri was a Ray. She was brave.
She would try again!

But the third class didn't go well AT ALL!
"Is something wrong?" Madame Adele asked her after class.
"I'm having a midlife crisis!" Zuri cried. "I *really* tried to like ballet, but this outfit, this hair! And I don't move like the other kids!"

"You don't have to move or *look* like everyone else to
be a dancer. Remember, dancing is all about imagination."
"REALLY?"
"Absolutely!" Madame Adele said.
And for the first time all week, Zuri was excited.

Back at home, Zuri was on a mission! She threw
open her dress-up trunk and looked for something
that screamed: I LIKE ME LIKE THIS!

"Too scary!"

"Too hot!"

"Too fancy!"

"Ahhh, perfect!"

Zuri trotted into class the next day feeling brand-new!
"That's not how a ballerina dresses!" Jessie said.
"Don't worry," Zuri whispered. "Dancing is all about imagination."

Madame Adele lined everyone up for the grand jeté.

The students leaped across the room, with pointed fingers and pointed toes.

Zuri wondered where the fun was in *that*.

GOAL!

Some students gulped. Some students clapped.
But not Jessie.

"Nice form, less shouting," Madame Adele said, smiling.

"Sorry," Zuri said.

The next move was a chassé.
The students swished and glided across the floor.
But Zuri thought her chassé could use some zing!

It was Zuri's best move yet.
But some students gasped. And some students cheered.
Madame Adele was impressed.
Jessie couldn't hold it in anymore.

"THERE'S NO SOCCER IN BALLET!!!"

Madame Adele paused the music.

"Both soccer and ballet require focus, technique, and dedication," she explained.

Then Madame Adele played a faster song. "How about we end class with something *extraordinary*? Let's dance in our own special way!"

A leaping twirl here. A flying kick there.
Happy, dancing students everywhere!
Everyone agreed: It was the best ballet
class ever!

Jessie apologized. "I'm sorry I got so upset, Zuri."
"And I'm sorry I didn't tell you I didn't like ballet," Zuri said.
"We don't always have to like the same things."
"But we can always find a way to make them fun . . ."

"Together!"

After their final ballet class, Jessie said, "It's your turn to pick next week's adventure. What do you want to try?" Zuri thought really hard.

"Oh! I've got an amazing idea!"
Jessie nodded. "I can make that work!"

The following week, it was time for art class. Zuri threw open her dress-up trunk and looked for something that screamed: I LIKE ME LIKE THIS! Even Sherlock Hound played along.

"Too spiky!"

"Too heavy!"

"Too sparkly!"

"Ahhh, perfect!"
Zuri would make artist Frida Kahlo proud.

Zuri waited for Jessie to arrive. She dreamed of all the masterpieces they would create!

DING! DONG!

"Coming!" Zuri rushed to the door.

"Jessie? Isn't it art class this week?"
"Yup! And we're blasting off in
three, two, one! Let's do this, Zuri!"

A C T I V

ART CLASS

Ballet
FOR BEGINNERS

GYMNASTICS
CAMP

MAD
SCIENCE

BE
CREATIVE

GARDENING
101